junie b. jones

and That Meanie Jim's Birthday

by BARBARA PARK

illustrated by

Denise Brunkus

Long tail Books

Contents

G H I J K L M N O

1
Eating Cake

My name is Junie B. Jones. The B **stand**s **for** Beatrice. **Except** I don't like Beatrice. I just like B and **that's all**.

B is my bestest[1] letter. **On account of** my favorite food starts with that guy.

Its name is birthday cake.

We had that delicious **stuff** at school

---

1 **bestest** 단어 'best(최고의)'를 강조한 비격식적인 표현. '최고로 좋은' 이라는 뜻을 나타내며 어린아이가 주로 사용한다.

today.

That's because Paulie Allen Puffer turned six years old. And his mother brought chocolate cake and chocolate ice cream and chocolate milk to Room Nine.

She is a chocolate **nut**, I think.

The party was very fun.

Except for Paulie Allen Puffer got all **wound up**. And he put cake on his head. And then he laughed till milk came out his nose.

"That is called nose milk," I told my bestest friend named Lucille.

Lucille is a little lady.

"Eew,[2]" she said. "I wish I didn't

---

2 eew '웩'이라는 뜻으로 역겨움을 나타내는 표현.

even see that nose milk. 'Cause now my **stomach** feels **upset**. And I can't eat the rest of my cake."

"Me too," I said. "Now I can't eat the rest of my cake, too. And so I will throw both our cakes in the **trash** can for us."

Then I picked up our cakes. And I hurried up to the trash can.

I looked all around me very **careful**.

Then I quick **duck**ed behind the trash can.

And I stuffed both those cakes right in my mouth.

I **rub**bed my **tummy** real happy.

"Now all I need is some milk to wash it down with," I said.

That's when I saw some milk sitting on a

table. All **by itself**.

I picked it up. And drank it all gone.

"Mmmm," I said. "That hit the **spot!**"

Just then, I heard a voice.

"Junie B. Jones? Why are you out of your seat?"

It was my teacher.

Her name is Mrs.

She has another name, too. But I just like Mrs. and that's all.

Mrs. has eyes like a **hawk**.[3]

"What are you doing over there?" she asked me.

"I am sharing people's cake and milk," I explained. "Except for they aren't actually

---

3 **have eyes like a hawk** '눈이 매와 같이 예리하다', '무엇이든 못 보고 놓치는 법이 없다'라는 뜻의 숙어.

here at the moment."

Mrs. **roll**ed **her eyes** way back in her head.

I smiled very sweet.

"Guess what? When I have *my* birthday party, I am going to bring cake and milk, too," I said. "Plus also, I might bring a beanie weenie[4] casserole.[5] 'Cause that will be a nice change of **pace**, I think."

Just then, I **skip**ped over to Paulie Allen Puffer's mother.

"Excellent cake, madam. My **compliment**s to the *chief*,[6]" I said.

---

4 **beanie weenie** 토마토소스에 넣어 삶은 강낭콩. 'Beanee Weenee'라는 제품명의 통조림으로 널리 소비된다.

5 **casserole** 캐서롤. 강낭콩과 여러 가지 고기를 오랫동안 쪄서 만드는 서양식 요리.

6 **my compliments to the chief** 맛있는 음식을 먹고 나서 전하는 인사 'my compliments to the chef(주방장에게 감사 인사를 전합니다)'에서 주니 B.가 'chef(주방장)'를 'chief(장, 우두머리)'로 잘못 말한 것이다.

Then me and her did a **high five**. Only she didn't actually put her hand out. And so mostly I just **slap**ped her on the arm.

After that, I skipped back to my seat.

Lucille was finishing her chocolate ice cream.

She had a chocolate **mustache** on her **lip**.

I did a **frown** at her.

"Lucille, I am surprised at you," I said. "You are not eating that ice cream like a little lady. And so I will show you how."

Then I quick **dip**ped my spoon into Lucille's ice cream.

"See?" I said. "See how I am taking **dainty bites** of this stuff?"

Only just then, a dainty bite of chocolate

ice cream **slip**ped off my spoon. And it **plop**ped into Lucille's **lap**.

She jumped out of her chair.

"OH NO!" she **holler**ed. "NOW LOOK WHAT YOU DID! YOU **SPILL**ED ICE CREAM ON MY **BRAND-NEW** DRESS! AND MY **NANNA** JUST BROUGHT THIS TO ME FROM NEW YORK CITY! AND IT COSTED[7] NINETY-FIVE DOLLARS PLUS **TAX**!"

Mrs. hurried up to my table. She had a wet sponge to clean Lucille's dress.

"No! Don't!" said Lucille. "You can't put water on this! 'Cause this dress is made of

---

7 **costed** (cost) 영어권 국가의 아이들이 동사의 과거형을 말할 때 모든 단어의 끝에 '-ed'를 붙이는 실수를 종종 한다. 이 책에 나오는 'hided (hid)', 'runned(ran)' 등이 이와 같은 경우이다.

E F G H I J K L M N O P

satin![8] And satin is dry clean[9] only!"

Mrs. made angry eyes at me.

I did a **gulp**.

"Who knew?" I said real soft.

Then I put my head down on my table.

And I **cover**ed up with my arms.

'Cause that is called laying low.

And laying low is what you do if you know what's good for you.

---

8 **satin** 새틴. 광택이 있고 매끄러운 천으로, 주로 장식적인 여성복, 핸드백, 모자 등에 사용된다.

9 **dry clean** 드라이클리닝. 물 대신 세탁용 유기화학제품으로 때를 빼는 세탁 방법. 물세탁을 할 수 없는 모직물, 실크 등의 세탁에 쓴다.

2
Tapping on That Jim's Head

After the party, me and my other bestest friend **rode** home on the bus.

Her name is Grace.

Me and that Grace take **turn**s sitting next to the window.

That is good sports of us, I think.

Except for sometimes we forget whose turn it is.

Then we have to **settle** it with our **fist**s.

This time, it was that Grace's turn to sit next to the window.

"Guess what? I don't even care if you sit there today," I told her. "'Cause eating all that cake made me in a happy **mood**."

That Grace smiled.

"Me too," she said. "Eating that cake made me in a happy mood, too."

"Yeah, only you can't be as happy as me," I explained. "'Cause I had two cakes. And you just had one."

That Grace did a **frown**.

"That's okay, Grace. Don't be **upset**," I said. "'Cause when I have my birthday, I will invite you to my house. And you can have two cakes, too."

"Oh boy![1]" she said.

"I know it is *oh boy*," I said back. "Plus also, you will get your very own paper cup with M&M's[2] in it."

"Ooooh! **Yum**! I *love* M&M's," said that Grace.

"Me too. I love M&M's, too," I said. "**On account of** the chocolate doesn't **melt** on your hands. Just the colors melt on your hands and **that's all**."

I smiled real big.

"And here's *another* good thing, Grace. When you come to my party, you will get your very own party hat. And we will play Twister.[3] Plus also, we will play that game

---

1 **boy** 여기에서는 '소년'이라는 뜻이 아니라, '맙소사' 또는 '어머나'라는 의미로 놀람이나 기쁨 등을 나타내는 표현으로 쓰였다.

2 **M&M's** 엠앤엠즈. 색소를 입혀 만든 작은 단추 크기의 초콜릿으로, 색상이 다양하며 앞부분에는 하얀색으로 소문자 'm'이 적혀 있다.

where you shout Bingo.[4] Only I keep on forgetting the name of that one."

Just then, a **meanie** boy named Jim jumped up from his seat.

"BINGO, stupid!" he shouted. "Its name is BINGO! What a **MORON**! Who would even want to come to a stupid party like yours?"

He made his voice real loud. So everybody could hear.

"At *my* house I have *cool* birthday parties," he said. "Like last year my party was named **Clown**ing Around. And we

---

3 **Twister** 트위스터. 여러 가지 색깔이 칠해진 판 위에 서서 회전판의 바늘이 가리키는 색깔에 두 손과 두 발을 올려 놓는 게임.

4 **Bingo** 빙고. 정방형의 표에 숫자를 여러 종류로 배열해 적고, 사회자가 임의로 부르는 숫자를 가장 빠르게 가로, 세로, 또는 사선으로 연결하는 것을 겨루는 게임.

had two clowns from the **circus**. And
they made balloon animals and did magic
tricks."

I **lean**ed way close to his face.

"So?" I said. "I don't even *like* clowns.
Clowns are not normal people. Plus my
very own grampa[5] Frank Miller can make
balloon animals, too. Except for they all
look like wiener dogs.[6] Only he's working
on it."

That Jim wasn't even listening to me.
He just kept on talking about his parties.

"*This* year my party is named Old
MacDonald's Farm. And a real farmer is

---

5 **grampa** '할아버지(grandpa)'를 부르는 말로, 'gramp', 'grampa',
'grampy' 등 다양한 표현이 있다.

6 **wiener dog** 닥스훈트(Dachshund). 개의 한 품종으로 허리가 길고 다
리가 짧은 것이 특징이다.

bringing a **pet**ting zoo right to my front
yard. And he's going to bring a **lamb**, and
a goat, and a **burro**, and some rabbits! And
he's also bringing a real, live **pony** for us
to ride!"

I put my hands on my **waist**.

"Yeah, well, too bad for you," I said.

"'Cause I saw all about ponies on TV. And ponies **buck** you off their backs. And then they **stomp**le[7] you into the ground and kill you to death. And so I wouldn't even come to your stupid **dumb** party in a **jillion billion** years."

"Good!" **holler**ed that Jim. "I'm glad! 'Cause my birthday is this coming Saturday! And tomorrow I'm bringing **invitation**s to every single person in Room Nine! Only *not* to you! You're the *only one* in the whole class I'm not bringing an invitation to! So there!"

Then he did a big HAH! right in my face.

---

7 **stomple** '쿵쿵거리며 짓밟다'라는 뜻으로 'stomp(쿵쿵거리며 걷다)'와 'trample(밟아뭉개다)'을 합쳐 만들어 낸 말.

And he sat back down in his seat.

Meanwhile, I just kept on standing and standing there.

'Cause something had gone a little bit wrong here, I think.

I tapped on his head.

"Yeah, only here's the thing," I said. "I didn't actually know you were having a party on Saturday. And so, good news . . . I think I can make it."

"No!" shouted that meanie boy. "You're not coming! Now go away!"

I tapped on him again.

"Yeah, only I was just **kid**ding about the ponies," I said. "They **hardly** even stomple you, probably."

"I don't care! Stop **bother**ing me!" he

shouted.

I stood on my **tippy-toe**s and looked at his head.

"Love your hair today," I said.

That Jim **swat**ted at me.

"Get away from me!" he hollered. "You're not coming to my party! And that's final!"

Just then, a big **lump** came in my **throat**. A big lump is what comes before crying.

It hurt to **swallow**.

I sat down and hided my face in my sweater.

"Darn it,[8]" I said. "'Cause I think I really would have enjoyed myself at that

---

8 **darn it** 'damn it(빌어먹을, 제기랄)'을 순화한 단어로, 못마땅하거나 짜증스러울 때 쓰는 숙어적 표현.

thing."

Then my bestest friend named Grace
put her arm around me.

And she **pat**ted me real gentle.

And she let me sit next to the window.

3
Very Slumping

I walked home from the bus stop very slumping.

Very slumping is when your **shoulder**s are sad. And your head can't hold up that good.

Grandma Miller was in the **nursery**.

She **baby-sit**s me and my baby brother in the afternoon.

His name is Ollie.

I love him a real lot. Except I wish he didn't live at my actual house.

Grandma Miller was **rock**ing him in the rocking chair.

I tried to climb up there, too. Only Grandma said "Hold your horses[1]" at me.

"Yeah, only I need to rock very bad," I explained. "On account of a **mean** boy is having a birthday party on Saturday. And he is inviting everyone in Room Nine. Only not me. I'm the *only one* who's not going."

Grandma Miller did a sad face.

"Children can be so **cruel**," she said. "Just wait till I get the baby to sleep. And

---

1 **hold one's horses** '기다려 봐', '잠깐 멈춰'라는 뜻의 숙어.

then you and I will talk about it. Okay?"

And so that's how come I **cross**ed **my arms**.

And I **tap**ped my foot.

And I waited and waited for that baby to go to sleep. Only his eyes kept on staying wide open.

"Hold them closed with your fingers, Grandma," I told her.

"**Heavens**, no!" she said.

Then she kept right on rocking him.

And so finally I got **tired** of waiting.

And I went to my room. And I **crawl**ed **underneath** my **cover**s.

I crawled way down to the bottom of my **sheet**s.

It is very **muffly**^{2} down there.

You can say mean **stuff**.

And no one can hear you.

"Here is all the stuff I hate," I said. "First, I hate that **meanie** Jim. Then I hate **clown**s. And Old MacDonald had a farmer. Plus I hate rabbits. And **burro**s. And **ponies**.

"And guess what else? We didn't actually need a baby at this house. Only no one even **consult**ed me."

Just then, I heard a **knock** on my door.

---

2 **muffly** 주니 B.가 만들어 낸 말로 단어 'muffle(소리를 죽이다)'의 뒤에 '-y'를 붙여 '조용한'이라는 의미의 형용사로 사용하였다. 이 책에 나오는 'stickery', 'pumpy'도 이와 같은 경우이다.

"Junie B.? It's Grandma, honey. Ollie finally went to sleep."

She came in and **lift**ed up my covers.

"I called your mother and told her what happened at school," she said.

I **peek**ed up at her.

"And so can she fix it?" I asked. "Can I go to the birthday party now?"

Grandma Miller held out her arms to me.

She pulled me out of my covers.

"Your mother is going to talk to you about it when she gets home," she said. "Meanwhile, why don't you and I have a little fun. Let's read a book, okay? What kind of story would you like to hear?"

I thought and thought.

"I would like to hear a story about a little girl who doesn't get invited to a meanie boy's birthday. And so she **sneak**s to his house. And she lets a wild pony out of the **barn**. And then it **stomp**les the boy into a **flat**tie pancake.[3] And all the children **pour** maple syrup[4] on that guy. And they eat him for breakfast."

Grandma Miller looked kind of **sickish**.

"You've got to stop worrying about that boy's party. He's just trying to get your goat,[5]" she said.

---

3 pancake 팬케이크. 밀가루에 달걀, 우유, 설탕을 한데 반죽하여 팬에서 구운 빈대떡 모양의 말랑한 케이크. 시럽을 뿌리거나 버터 등을 올려 먹는다.

4 maple syrup 메이플 시럽. 단풍나무의 수액을 졸여서 만든 밝은 갈색이 나는 시럽. 시럽은 과자나 음료를 만들 때 사용하거나 음식에 뿌려 먹는 걸쭉하고 달콤한 액체를 말한다.

5 **get one's goat** '화나게 하다', '약 올리다'라는 뜻의 숙어.

Just then, my eyes got big and wide at her.

"Goat? What goat, Grandma? Do I have a goat? Is it a surprise goat? Are you keeping it a secret at your house?"

I jumped up and pulled her hand.

"Let's go get it! Want to, Grandma? Let's go get my goat right now!"

Just then, a great idea **pop**ped in my head.

"HEY! I JUST THOUGHT OF SOMETHING, GRANDMA! YOU AND ME CAN BRING MY GOAT TO MY HOUSE! AND THEN I CAN HAVE MY VERY OWN BIRTHDAY ON SATURDAY!

"I WILL CALL IT 'COME AND **PET** MY GOAT'! AND EVERYONE IN ROOM

NINE WILL COME TO *MY* PARTY! AND THEY WON'T GO TO THAT MEANIE JIM'S!"

All of a sudden, the front door opened.

It was Mother!

I runned to her **speedy** quick.

"Mother! Mother! Guess what? Guess what? Me and Grandma Miller are getting my goat! And I am having my very own birthday party on Saturday! And all of Room Nine is going to be invited. Only not that Jim I hate! He is the *only one* not coming! So ha ha on him!"

Just then, Grandma Miller sneaked out the front door with her sweater.

I pulled on Mother's arm.

"Come on, Mother! Come on!" I said.

"We have to go to the store and buy my **invitation**s! Plus also, we have to pick up the beanie weenies!"

Mother didn't come on.

She sat down on the **couch**. And **smooth**ed my hair.

"Listen to me, Junie B.," she said. "I know Jim hurt your feelings today. But you can't have your birthday party on Saturday. Your birthday isn't till June, remember? And June is still months away."

"I know June is months away," I said. "And so that is how come I am moving my birthday sooner. 'Cause months away will be too late."

Mother picked me up and put me on

her **lap**.

"I'm afraid you don't understand, honey," she said. "You just can't *change* the day you were **born**. No one can. It's **impossible**."

I made my voice very **whisper**ing.

"Yeah, only here's a little secret . . . nobody in Room Nine even knows when my birthday is. So I think we can **pull** it **off**."

Mother did a little smile. She **ruffle**d my hair.

"Sorry, honey. No can do," she said.

"Yes!" I hollered. "Yes can do! 'Cause I *have* to have my birthday on Saturday! Or else I will be the *only one* who is not going to that meanie Jim's! And that is the saddest story I ever even heard of."

Just then, my eyes got a little bit of wet in them.

Mother **wipe**d my face with a **tissue**.

Then she **hug**ged me real tight.

And she said the words *I'm sorry.*

More bad news.

Grandma Miller just called . . .

There's no goat.

4
Moving

The next morning, I didn't get out of my bed.

Not even when Mother **holler**ed, "Time for breakfast."

She came into my room.

"Didn't you hear me, Junie B.? It's time to eat," she said.

I looked up from my **pillow**.

"Yeah, only I'm not even hungry. Plus

also, I'm moving today," I said.

Mother smiled.

She sat on my bed.

"You're moving, huh?" she asked. "And **exact**ly where will you be going?"

I did my **shoulder**s up and down.

"Somewhere," I said.

"Somewhere, where?" she asked.

"Somewhere not here, that's where," I said.

Mother **hug**ged me.

"This is still about Jim's birthday party, isn't it?" she said. "You're still worried about not getting an invitation."

"No, I'm not," I said. **"On account of** I'm not even going to that school anymore. On account of I'm moving today."

Mother shook her head. Then she went
out of my room. And she and Daddy did
whispering in the **hall**.

Pretty soon, Daddy came in.

He gave me a piggyback **ride**[1] to the

---

1 **piggyback ride** 업기 또는 목말 태우기. 등에 업어 주거나 업히는 것
을 뜻한다.

kitchen.

Then Mother made my favorite hot cereal.

And she let me have all the brown sugar I wanted.

She sat down next to me.

"You know, Junie B., Jim is only doing this to hurt your feelings," she said. "He just wants to get a **react**ion from you, **that's all**."

"Sure, he does," said Daddy. "And when someone is trying to hurt your feelings, there's only one way to get back at them."

"You have to **pretend** you don't care," said Mother. "You have to pretend you don't even *want* to go to that party. Because if you pretend you don't want to go, it will take all the fun out of it for him."

Daddy **wink**ed.

"You can do that, can't you?" he asked. "You're the best little pretender in the **entire** *world*."

Just then, my whole face **light**ed up. 'Cause that word gave me a great idea!

"Hey! I just **figure**d **out** where I can move to! It's called It's a Small World After All.[2] And it's at Disneyland![3] 'Member that, Daddy? It's where all those **puppet**s keep on singing that same song over and over

---

2 **It's a Small World After All** 주니 B.가 디즈니랜드의 놀이기구인 'It's a Small World'를 가리키는 것으로, 놀이기구를 타는 동안 'It's a small world after all'이라는 가사가 계속해서 흘러나온다.

3 **Disneyland** 디즈니랜드. 미국 캘리포니아주(州) 남서부에 있는 세계 최고 수준의 유원지. 미국의 만화 영화 제작자 월트 디즈니(Walt Disney)가 계획하여 건축하였다.

and over again."

I smiled. "That would be a happy place to live, don't you think?"

Daddy looked at me a real long time.

Then he put his head down on the table. And he started **knock**ing it on the **edge**.

Mother pulled him up from there.

They went in the hall and did more whispering.

After a while, Mother called to me from her bedroom.

"Junie B.? Could you pick up the phone, please? It's your grandfather. He wants to talk to you for a minute."

I picked up the phone. "H'lo?"

"Hello yourself, little girl," said my

grampa Frank Miller. "What'cha **up to** this morning?"

"I'm moving today," I told him.

Grampa Miller sounded **upset**.

"Moving?" he said. "Oh no! You *can't* be moving! If you move, then you won't be able to come over to my house on Saturday!"

I **crinkle**d up my **eyebrow**s at him.

'Cause this **conversation** smelled **fishy**, that's why.

"Yeah, only how come you want me to come to your house?" I asked. "And how come it has to be on Saturday?"

"Because Saturday's the day I do my work around here, remember?" he said. "You're still my little helper, aren't you?"

I thought very **careful**.

"Yes," I said.

On account of sometimes I help Grampa fix stuff. It is called **odd** jobs, I think.

"Are you doin' odd jobs?" I asked him. "Is that why you want me to come there?"

"Sure I'm doin' odd jobs," said my grampa. "But I can't do them without my helper, can I? You're the one who wears the **tool** belt, aren't you?"

I smiled very **proud**. 'Cause Grampa Miller's tool belt is the bestest thing I love. It has a **jillion** tools hanging off of that thing. It **wrap**s around me two whole times. And I don't even **cave in**.

Just then, Grampa Miller made his voice real quiet.

"You haven't even heard the best part yet," he whispered. "Guess what I'm going to be fixing?"

I whispered back at him. "What?"

Then Grampa said for me to **hang on** a minute. On account of he wanted to close his door. Or else my grandma might hear.

"If your grandma hears, then *she'll* want to be my helper, **instead** of you," he said.

I waited very **patient**.

"Ready?" he said.

"Ready," I said.

"Okay. I'm going to be fixing the **upstairs** *toilet*."

Just then, my mouth came **all the way** open.

'Cause fixing the upstairs toilet is a

dream come true, that's why!

"Are you gonna take the **lid** off the top, Grampa? And are you gonna keep **flush**ing it and flushing it? And are you gonna watch all the water go out of that thing?" I asked.

"Sure I am! Of course I am! That's half the fun of fixing the toilet! Right?" he said.

"Right!" I said very excited. "Plus also, I love that big ball that **float**s on the top."

"Me too!" said my grampa. "I love that big ball, too! And so I can **count on** you, can't I? You and I have a **date** on Saturday, right?"

I thought some more.

"Yeah, only I think there's something you forgot, Grampa."

"What?" he asked. "What did I forget, little girl?"

I raised my eyebrows at that **silly**head.

"You forgot that I'm moving today."

5
Being a Buzzing Bee

Grandma and Grampa Miller take **turn**s **baby-sit**ting me before lunch. Then they get me dressed for **kindergarten**.

Except for today, Mother came home from work. And she got me dressed **instead**.

She said she would drive me to school.

"If I drive you, then you won't have to see Jim on the bus," she said very

thoughtful.

She got out my clothes for school.

It was my jumper[1] with the frogs on it.

"Yeah, only guess what? I'm not even wearing school clothes today. On account of I'm moving. And so I have to wear moving man clothes."

Mother kept on trying to put that jumper on me.

That's how come I made my legs and arms real **stiff**. So they wouldn't **fit** in there that good.

Then me and Mother **wrestle**d a **teeny** bit. And she stood me on my head. And

---

1 **jumper** 여기에서는 외투가 아닌 '점퍼스커트'를 가리키는 말로 사용되었다. 점퍼스커트는 블라우스나 티셔츠 위에 입는 소매가 없는 원피스이다.

she pulled my tights[2] on me.

"You're not moving, Junie B.," she said. "You're going to school, and that's final. Running away from your problems never solves anything."

"Yeah, only I'm not even running," I said. "I'm calling Ryder Rents Trucks. And those guys will drive me."

Mother smiled. She tried to hug me. But I kept on staying real stiff.

I stayed real stiff **all the way** in the car to school.

Mother parked the car in the **parking lot**.

Then she **lift**ed me out the door. And

---

2 **tights** 타이츠. 주로 어린이들이 방한용으로 신는, 허리까지 오는 긴 양말.

she carried me real stiff to the **playground**.

She stood me up in the grass.

"Everything will be fine. You'll see," she said. "Just remember what Daddy and I told you. If anyone talks about the party, **pretend** it doesn't **bother** you."

She kissed me goodbye on my stiff head.

Just then, I heard voices hollering.

"JUNIE B.! HEY, JUNIE B.! LOOK! LOOK WHAT WE GOT!" they hollered.

I turned around.

It was my bestest friends, Lucille and that Grace. They were running at me.

"Look!" said Lucille. "Look what Jim gave us! It's **invitation**s to his birthday party on Saturday!"

"It's just like he told us, Junie B.!" said that Grace. "He's really gonna have a **pet**ting zoo there!"

I quick **cover**ed my ears with my hands.

Then I closed my eyes. And I sang a loud song at them.

It is called "I Can't Hear You, You're Not Even Botherin' Me."

I sang it at the top of my **lung**s.[3]

"I CAAA-ANNN'T HEARRRR YOU!

"I CAAA-ANNN'T HEARRRR YOU!

"YOU'RE NOT E-VEN BOTHERIN' MEEEE!"

Then I kept on singing and singing that

---

3 **at the top of one's lungs** '큰 소리로', '목청껏'이라는 뜻의 숙어.

thing till they went away.

Also, they did the cuckoo sign[4] at me.

After that, I sat down in the grass all
by myself. And I looked all around the
playground.

Lots of other children had invitations,
too.

"Darn it," I whispered. "Darn it. Darn it.
Darn it."

That's when I saw that **meanie** Jim.

He was giving an invitation to a boy
named **Crybaby** William.

Crybaby William is the **scarediest cat**[5]
in Room Nine.

---

4 **cuckoo sign** '미쳤다'라는 의미로 관자놀이 주변에서 손가락을 빙빙
돌리는 행동을 말한다.

5 **scarediest cat** 'scaredy cat(순 겁쟁이)'라는 단어의 'scaredy'를 주니
B.가 최상급처럼 강조하여 말했다.

He is even **scare**d of a teeny **flea**, I
think.

Just then, I sat up a little bit straighter.

'Cause I just got another idea in my
head, that's why!

It was called, Hey! Maybe I can take
William's invitation away from him! 'Cause
he won't even **chase** me, probably! And so
then I will have my very own invitation!
And William can get another one from that
Jim! And then *everybody* will get to go to
the party. **Including** me!

I stood up from the grass.

Then I **squint**ed my eyes at Crybaby
William. And I started to run at him very
slow.

I runned faster and faster. Till finally,

I was running as fast as a **speed**ing bumblebee.[6]

I buzzed all around William **zippity**[7] quick.

His eyes couldn't even follow me that good.

Then I buzzed right in his face. And I quick **grab**bed that invitation out of his fingers!

I runned my fastest to the **swing** set!

And guess what?

William didn't even follow me! That's what!

And here's more good news! William's

---

6 **bumblebee** 호박벌. 몸에 검은색과 노란색 털이 난 꿀벌과의 곤충.

7 **zippity** 단어 'zippy(아주 빠른)'를 강조하여 말한 것으로, 'zippity quick'은 '아주 빠르게'라는 뜻의 비격식적 표현이다.

invitation didn't even have his name on
it! So that means it can be for *anybody*,
probably!

"Only now it's mine!" I said. "'Cause
I will put my name on it when I get to
Room Nine! And it will be my very own

invitation!"

Just then, the bell rang for school.

I put my invitation way down in my deep pocket. And I **skip**ped very happy to my class.

Mrs. was standing outside of Room

Nine.

William was standing with her.

His nose was **sniffling** a real lot.

I tried to skip past them. But Mrs.
grabbed the **strap**s of my frog jumper.

She pulled me back.

"Yeah, only I don't actually think that is
good for the **outfit**," I said.

Mrs. did a **frown**.

"Junie B., did you take something that
belonged to William?" she asked.

"No," I said. "'Cause his name wasn't
even on it. And so that means it is for
anybody, I think."

Mrs. **tap**ped her angry foot.

"Was William *holding* an invitation,
Junie B.? And did you **snatch** it out of his

hands? And then did you run away from him?" she asked.

I smiled very cute.

"I was a buzzing bee," I said.

Mrs. holded out her hand.

"May I have it, please?" she asked. "May I have the invitation you took from William?"

I **rock**ed **back and forth** on my feet.

'Cause I didn't want to give it to her, that's why.

"Yeah, only I think it mighta[8] **bounce**d out of my pocket," I said.

Mrs. **bend**ed down next to me. She **lean**ed way into my face.

---

8 **mighta** 'might have'를 발음대로 쓴 표현.

"I want that invitation," she said.
"Now."

I did a **gulp**.

Then I quick put my hand in my pocket.

"Good news. I found it," I said very nervous.

"Give it to William," said Mrs.

Crybaby William put out his hand.

I **shove**d it at him.

"Here, Mr. **Stinky**head **Tattletale** Boy," I said. "Here's your stinkyhead invitation."

Mrs.'s eyes got real big.

"Junie B. Jones! That's quite enough! Now you go sit down! And I don't want to hear another word. Do you understand, young lady? Not one more word."

And so that's how come I walked very

slumping to my seat.

And I put my head on my table.

'Cause guess why?

Laying low again, that's why.

6
Daydreaming

Mrs. took **attendance**. Attendance is when you say, *I'm here.* **Except** if you're not here, you have to be quiet.

Also, we said, *I **pledge allegiance** to the **flag** of the United States of America.*[1]

That is called opening **ceremonies**, I think.

---

1 **I pledge allegiance. . . of America** 미국의 국기에 대한 맹세. 우리 나라에서 하듯이 오른손을 왼쪽 가슴 위에 얹고 말한다.

After that, we sat down. And Mrs.
passed out our workbooks.

She told us the pages to turn to.

It was work about different kinds of
shapes. Like circles. And **squares**. And
triankles.[2]

I am a **breeze** at that **stuff**.

Only I couldn't even **concentrate** very
good. **On account of** I kept daydreaming
about that birthday party.

Daydreaming is just like night dreaming.

Only it's not night.

And you're not **asleep**.

And you're not dreaming.

I kept on thinking about how everybody

---

2 **triankle** 단어 'triangle(삼각형)'을 잘못 말한 것이다.

was going to that party.

Only not me.

I was the *only one*.

In *all* of Room Nine.

I wish Lucille and Grace weren't going, too, I thought to just myself. *'Cause that would be nice sports of them.*

After a while, I tapped on Lucille.

"You are my bestest good friend," I told her.

Lucille smiled at me.

"You are my bestest good friend, too," she said.

I touched her new dress.

"You look very **precious** today," I said.

Lucille **fluff**ed herself.

"Thank you. You look very precious

today, too," she said back.

I touched her **fingernail**s with **polish** on them.

"I wish you and me could be **twin**s," I said.

"Me too. I wish you and me could be twins, too," she said.

Just then, my whole face got happy.

"Lucille! Lucille! I just thought of something! You and me can *pretend* we are twins! And we can do everything just the same! And so on Saturday you can come to my house. And I will put **nail** polish on my nails, just like you! And you will stay home from that birthday party, just like me!"

Lucille didn't say anything back.

I tapped on her.

"How come you're not talking, twin?" I said. "How come you're not saying anything back?"

"'Cause I want to go to the party, that's why," said Lucille.

I did a **huffy** breath at her.

"Yes, Lucille. I *know* you want to go to the party. But now you and me are twins. And twins have to do everything just the same. And so if *I* don't go to the party, then *you* can't go to the party, too. On account of that is the twin **rule**s."

"No, it's not," said Lucille. "My **cousin**s are twins. And one is a boy. And one is a girl. And they don't do *anything* alike."

I jumped up from my chair.

"Yeah, only that is not the kind of twin I want to be, madam!³" I **yell**ed.

Mrs. **snap**ped her loud fingers at me.

"Sit down!" she **holler**ed.

Just then, that Jim I hate turned around in his chair. And he laughed real **mean** at me. 'Cause I was in trouble.

"Turn around your fatty head!" I said.

Only he didn't turn it around. And so that's how come I had to run to his table. And I had to turn it around for him.

"JUNIE B. JONES!" shouted Mrs. "WHAT ARE YOU DOING?"

"I am turning around his fatty head," I explained.

3　**madam** '계집애'라는 뜻으로 건방진 여자아이를 얕잡아 부를 때 사용하는 비격식적인 호칭.

Mrs. hurried to where I was. Then she quick took my arm. And she **march**ed me into the **hall**.

She pointed to **Principal**'s office.

"Go!" she said real angry.

I did a **gulp**.

"Yeah, only I**'m** not actually **supposed to** go there anymore," I said. "'Cause me and Mother had a talk about it. And she said for me not to get sent there again."

Mrs.'s face got red as a tomato.

She started **count**ing numbers.

"One . . . two . . . three . . . four . . ."

And so that's how come I hurried up and walked.

'Cause teachers who count numbers are the **scariest** kind there is.

7
My Story This Time
by Junie B. Jones

Principal is the boss of the school.

He lives at the office.

I have to go there when I am **unruly**.

Unruly is the school word for not being ruly.

There is a **typing** lady there. She isn't allowed to smile.

"Sit down," she said.

She pointed at the blue chair.

"Yeah, only I don't actually like to sit there, remember that? 'Cause that is where the bad kids sit. And I am not even bad," I explained.

I explain that to her every time I go there.

The typing lady **lean**ed over the **counter** at me. She made her face look **scary** at me.

"Sittttt dowwwwn," she said.

I sat down.

Then I pulled my frog jumper over my face. So nobody could see me.

"Pull your skirt back down," said the typing lady.

"Yeah, only I'm actually allowed to do this. 'Cause I have on tights," I said. "See them? They are green with little **tadpole**s on them."

Just then, I heard Principal's voice.

"Well, well . . . Junie B. Jones. What a surprise," he said.

My mouth dropped **all the way** opened.

"HEY!" I hollered from under my dress. "HOW DID YOU KNOW IT'S ME UNDER HERE? 'CAUSE YOU CAN'T EVEN SEE MY FACE!"

"Lucky guess," said Principal.

After that, I **uncover**ed my head. And me and him went in his office.

I climbed up in the big wood chair.

Principal looked very tiredish.[1] He

---

1 **tiredish** 주니 B.가 만들어 낸 말로 단어 'tired(피곤한)'의 뒤에 '-ish'를 붙여 '피곤한 듯한', '피곤한 것 같은'이라는 의미의 형용사로 사용하였다.

rubbed the sides of his **baldie** head.

"Okay, let's hear it. What's your story this time?" he said.

I sat up straight and tall.

"My Story This Time, by Junie B. Jones.

"Once upon a time, I didn't get invited to a **meanie** boy's birthday. And I am the *only one* in *all* of Room Nine who isn't going. And so that's how come I was moving today. Only Mother brought me to school very **stiff**. And then I was a **buzz**ing bee. Only **Crybaby** William is a **squeal**er. And Lucille won't be a good **twin**. And so then Mrs. **yell**ed at me. And that's how come I had to **twist** that Jim's head. And now I am sitting here in this big wood chair."

I **fold**ed my hands on my **lap**.

"The end."

Principal put his head down on his desk.

I **peek**ed at him.

"Are you laying low?" I **whisper**ed.

He sat up again. Then he called my mother on the telephone.

Those two talk very often.

This time, they talked about the birthday party. And how I'm not invited.

After he **hang**ed **up**, Principal looked nicer at me.

"I guess sometimes we **grown-up**s think we're the only ones with problems," he said. "We forget that even when you're little, life can be **tough**. Can't it, Junie B.

Jones?"

"Yes," I said. "Life can get your goat."

After that, me and him went out of his office. And he **lift**ed me into the blue chair again.

"I want you to wait here a minute," he said. "There's someone I have to talk to before I can get this **settle**d."

"Yeah, only guess what? I don't actually want to sit in this chair," I explained. "On account of this is where the bad kids sit. And I'm not even bad."

Principal thought and thought. Then he **snap**ped his fingers.

"I think I might have the perfect solution," he said.

He went in his office and brought out a

giant shopping bag.

"What if we hide you under here?" he asked. "If we hide you under this bag, no one will be able to see you at all."

I jumped up and down very excited. 'Cause hiding is my favorite thing in the whole world, that's why!

Principal sat me down in the chair.

He put that giant shopping bag over my head.

"HEY! WHO TURNED OUT THE LIGHTS?" I said.

Then I laughed and laughed. 'Cause that is called *comedy*, of course.

I **bend**ed my **knee**s and pulled them under the bag. I **hug**ged them real tight.

"Now all you can see is the **tippy-toe**s of

my shoes!" I said very happy.

"This is the perfectest[2] solution I ever saw! And so how did you even think of this wonderful thing?" I asked.

Only Principal didn't answer me back.

'Cause he probably went back to his office already.

After that I hided and hided inside my bag.

I hided a real long time.

It was a **jillion** years, I think.

"Guess what? This is taking longer than a minute," I said from inside there.

The typing lady didn't answer me.

"Yeah, only guess what else? My knees are very bended and **squish**ed in here," I said. "And so this isn't good for my **circlelation**,[3] probably."

Just then, my legs started **squirm**ing all

---

2 **perfectest** '가장 완벽한'이라는 뜻을 지닌 비격식적인 표현. 원래는 단어 'perfect'가 '완벽한'이라는 의미를 나타내기 때문에 형용사의 최상급을 만드는 부사인 'most'를 잘 붙이지 않는다.

3 **circlelation** 단어 'circulation(혈액순환)'을 잘못 말한 것이다.

around. 'Cause I was getting ants in my
pants,[4] that's why!

"HEY! DOESN'T ANYBODY HAVE
EARS? GET ME OUTTA HERE RIGHT
NOW! 'CAUSE I AM AT THE END OF
MY ROPE[5] IN THIS THING! PLUS ALSO, I
AM GETTING ANTS IN MY . . ."

All of a sudden, someone **yank**ed the
bag right off my head.

It was the scary typing lady.

". . . pants," I said very soft.

She took me back into Principal's office.

And guess what?

That Jim was in there!

---

4 **get ants in one's pants** ‘초조해하다’, ‘안절부절못하다’라는 뜻의 숙
   어.

5 **at the end of one's rope** ‘막다른 지경에 이르러’, ‘한계에 이르러’라
   는 뜻의 숙어.

He was sitting in the big wood chair!

And Principal was **frown**ing at him!

"Junie B., our friend Jim here has something he wants to say to you. Don't you, Jim?" asked Principal.

That meanie Jim didn't answer. He kept on looking at his feet.

Principal **tap**ped his fingers.

"We're *waiting*, Jim," he said.

Then that Jim did a **huffy** breath. And he said the words *I'm sorry*.

Principal raised up his **eyebrow**s.

"Sorry for what, Jim? Tell Junie B. what you're sorry for."

That Jim **stare**d at his feet some more.

"I'm sorry I didn't give her an **invitation** to my party," he said very **grumpity**.[6]

"But your mother *told* you to, didn't she, Jim?" said Principal. "Your mother told you to give an invitation to every single person in your class. But you got mad at Junie B. And you decided not to give her one. Isn't that right?"

That meanie boy did his **shoulder**s up and down.

"I guess," he said real soft.

Principal **cross**ed **his arms**.

"And so what are you going to do to **correct** the problem?" he asked.

That Jim waited and waited.

Then—all of a sudden—he got down from his chair.

---

6 **grumpity** 단어 'grumpy(기분이 언짢은)'를 강조하여 말한 표현.

And he holded out an invitation to me.

My **stomach** did a **flip**py **flop**.[7]

"For me? Is that really for me!" I said

---

7 flippy flop '공중제비'라는 뜻의 단어 'flip flop'을 주니 B.가 'flippy flop'이라고 장난스럽게 말한 표현.

very squealing.

Then I **snatch**ed that thing right out of his hand. And I **zoom**ed all around the room.

"Oh boy!" I said. "It's really for me! It's really for me! And so now I'm not the *only one!*"

I zoomed all around the big wood chair. Principal looked nervous of me.

He hurried up and opened his door.

Then I zoomed right out of there!

And I didn't stop till I got to Room Nine!

8
Ruining My Saturday

On Saturday, Mother woke me up from sleeping.

"We have to go to the store and buy Jim a present," she said.

I did a sleepy **yawn**.

"Yeah, only I don't actually like that boy," I explained. "And so you can go **by yourself**. And I will trust your **judgment**."

I pulled the **cover**s over my head.

Mother pulled them off again.

Then she made me get dressed.

And she made me eat a banana.

And she made me go to the store with her.

She holded my hand and pulled me behind her.

"Since we don't know what he already has, let's get him something **unusual**," she said.

"Let's get him **greasy, grimy gopher guts**.[1] That is unusual," I said.

Mother made a sick face.

She pulled me through the store.

---

1 **greasy, grimy gopher guts** 노래 'Great Green Gobs of Greasy, Grimy Gopher Guts'의 가사 일부. '기름투성이의 더러운 땅다람쥐 내장'이라는 뜻이지만, 뜻보다는 두운에 초점을 맞추어 부르는 노래이다.

We went past the bathroom **stuff**.

I pointed.

"*That*. Let's get him *that*," I said. "*That* is unusual."

Mother **suck**ed in her **cheek**s.

"We're not getting him a **toilet brush**," she said.

She pulled me past the **pet** stuff.

"*That*. Let's get him *that*," I said. "*That* is unusual."

But Mother said, "No **choke chain**."

Just then, she pulled me past the **tool**s.

That's when my eyes **pop**ped right out of my head!

"THAT! LET'S GET HIM THAT! LOOK, MOTHER! LOOK! I LOVE THAT THING!"

I runned to it **speedy** quick.

"IT'S A TOOL BELT! SEE? IT'S JUST
LIKE GRAMPA MILLER'S! ONLY IT'S
MADE FOR LITTLE CHILDREN LIKE
ME! SEE IT, MOTHER? SEE THIS
WONDERFUL THING!"

Mother took it down off the **shelf**.

"Look!" I said. "It has a **hammer**! And
a **screwdriver**! And some **plier**s! And a
flashlight! And a real actual level^2 with a
bubble in it! Plus also, there's a pocket with
little **pretend nail**s in the front."

I jumped all around.

"Can I try it on? Can I? Please, Mother?
Please? Please?"

---

2 **level** 수준기 또는 수평기. 수평선이나 수평면을 측정하기 위한 기구로,
여기에서는 관에 들어 있는 기포의 중심을 눈금의 중심에 맞추어 수평을
구하는 기포 수준기를 가리킨다.

Mother shook her head no.

"We're not shopping for you today, Junie B. We're shopping for Jim, remember?"

"I know it. I know we are shopping for that Jim," I said. "And so this can be for his birthday. Only first I have to try it on to see if it **fit**s. 'Cause him and me are both the same size, I **bet**!"

Finally, Mother **fasten**ed the tool belt on me.

"Ooooh! It has Velcro![3]" I said. "I love this stickery stuff! Can we buy it? Please, Mother? Can we buy it? And take it home to my house?"

---

3 **Velcro** 벨크로. 흔히 우리가 찍찍이라고 부르는 것으로, 옷이나 신발 등의 두 폭을 한데 떼었다 붙였다 하는 데 주로 사용된다.

Mother thought and thought.

"I don't know, Junie B. Something tells me this isn't a good idea. I'm afraid you'll want to keep it."

"No, I won't! I won't want to keep it. I promise, Mother! I promise! I promise!"

And so finally Mother **gave in** to me. And she bought the wonderful tool belt.

I held it on my lap **all the way** home in the car.

Then I runned into the house. And I **zoom**ed to my room. And I put that thing on me again.

"Now I can do **odd** jobs!" I said real **thrill**ed.

I took the hammer and **tap**ped on my wall.

Then I **screw**ed a screw with the

screwdriver.

Plus also, I **twist**ed my Teddy's[4] nose off

---

4 **Teddy** 어린아이들이 장난감 곰 인형 테디 베어(teddy bear)를 부를
때 사용하는 애칭.

with the pliers. Only I actually didn't mean to do that one.

I **pat**ted his head.

"**Breathe** through your mouth," I said.

Just then, Mother's voice **holler**ed to me.

"JUNIE B.! IT'S TIME TO TAKE YOUR BATH, HONEY!"

I did a **frown**. 'Cause Mother was a little **mixed up**, I think.

I hollered back.

"YEAH, ONLY I DON'T EVEN HAVE TO TAKE A BATH TODAY! **ON ACCOUNT OF** TODAY IS SATURDAY! AND SATURDAY IS MY DIRTY DAY!"

Mother came in my room.

"I *know* today is Saturday, Junie B.," she said. "But you're going to a birthday party.

And when you go to a birthday party, you have to take a bath. Plus we're going to have to wash and **curl** your hair."

I backed up from her.

"No," I said. "'Cause nobody even explained that to me before. And so that doesn't even **make sense**. On account of I hate that meanie kid. So how come I have to get clean for him?"

Mother looked at the end of her rope.

"When you go to a party, you take a bath. **Period**. End of **discuss**ion," she said.

Then she left my room. And she went to start the **tub**.

I sat on my bed very **glum**.

"Darn it," I said. "'Cause that stupid boy is ruining my whole **entire** Saturday."

Mother hollered some more.

"JUNIE B.? COULD YOU BRING ME THE TOOL BELT, PLEASE? I NEED TO GET IT **WRAP**PED!"

"Darn it," I said again.

'Cause I didn't even want to give that to him.

I looked down at it.

I touched all the wonderful tools.

"I love this darned[5] thing," I said real sad.

"I'M WAITING!" shouted Mother.

But I still didn't take it to her.

Just then, I heard the bath water turn off.

---

5 **darned** 'damn(빌어먹을)'을 순화한 단어로, 못마땅하거나 짜증스러울 때 쓰는 표현.

My heart got very **pump**y.

"Oh no!" I said. "'Cause now she's gonna come get me! And she will take my tool belt away! And she will wrap it up for that meanie guy!"

I jumped off my bed and runned around my room.

"I gotta hide! I gotta hide!"

I runned all over everywhere.

"Darn it! 'Cause there's not even a good hiding place in this **dumb** room!" I said.

"JUNIE B.!" Mother **scream**ed.

I heard her feet!

They were coming for me, I think!

"Oh no!" I said. "Oh no! Oh no!"

Then **all of a sudden**, I quick **grab**bed my wonderful tool belt!

And I zoomed to my door!

And I tried to nail that thing shut with my hammer!

9
The Only One
in Room Nine

Mother runned into my room.

'Cause **pretend nail**s don't actually work, **apparent**ly.

"JUNIE B. JONES! WHAT IN THE WORLD ARE YOU DOING IN HERE?" she shouted.

She looked at my door.

Her eyes got very **bulging**.

"YOU WERE *HAMMER*ING?" she

yelled. "YOU WERE TRYING TO
HAMMER *NAILS*??? . . . IN YOUR
DOOR?"

Just then, Daddy runned in, too.

"WHERE IN THE WORLD DID YOU
GET A HAMMER?" he yelled.

"Tell him, Junie B.! Tell your father
where you got the hammer!" **growl**ed
Mother.

I pointed at her.

"*She* gave it to me," I said.

Just then, **steam** came out of Mother's
head.

"NO! I DID *NOT* GIVE YOU THAT
HAMMER, JUNIE B.! THAT HAMMER
WAS FOR JIM! AND YOU KNOW IT!"

After that, Mother picked me up. And

she sat me on my bed. And she growled more mad words at me.

They were . . . I cannot be trusted to have a real actual hammer. And I cannot be trusted to have a real actual **tool** belt. And I am never, ever allowed to have nails until I am all **grown-up** and I live in my own apartment.

Daddy walked up and down in front of me.

"Why, Junie B.? Why would you do such a thing? Why would you ever try to nail your door shut?" he said.

I started to cry a little bit.

"Because," I said.

"Because *why*?" he **grouch**ed.

"Because I felt **pressure** inside me," I

said. "Because that party is **ruin**ing my whole **entire** Saturday. Because first I had to shop. And then Mother said I had to get a bath and wash my hair. Only I don't even *like* that **meanie** head boy. And so how come I have to get clean and give him that wonderful tool belt? 'Cause what kind of **deal** is that?"

Mother did an angry breath.

"This was *your* decision, Junie B.," she said. "*You're* the one who wanted to go to the party. No one is making you do it."

I **wipe**d my nose on my sweater **sleeve**.

"Yeah, only if I don't go, I will be the *only one* in Room Nine," I said. "And that is the saddest story I ever heard of."

Daddy sat down next to me.

"Why?" he said. "Why is it sad to spend your Saturday the way *you* want to spend it? Why is it sad to spend the day having *fun*, **instead** of wasting it on a boy you don't like?"

Mother sat down, too.

"That doesn't sound sad to me," said Mother. "That sounds *good*, in fact."

"No, that does *not* sound good," I said very **snap**ping. "What is so good about being the *only one*?"

Daddy did his **shoulder**s up and down.

"Lots of things," he said. "Like you'll be the *only one* who doesn't have to take a bath. Have you ever thought of that?"

"And you'll be the *only one* who doesn't have to wash her hair," said Mother.

"And," said Daddy, "you'll be the *only*
one in Room Nine who doesn't have to give
Jim a present. How 'bout *that* one? Huh?"

I sat up a little bit straighter.

'Cause *that* one was excellent, that's why.

Mother **ruffle**d my hair.

"And what about Grampa Miller?" she
asked. "You haven't forgotten that he
invited you to his house today, have you?"

Just then, my whole mouth came open.

'Cause I *did* forget about that!

"The **toilet**!" I said. "I forgot about the
toilet! 'Cause me and Grampa were going
to fix that thing! And we were going to
touch that big ball that **float**s on top!"

Mother **made a face**.

"Lovely," she said.

"I *know* it is lovely," I said. "And so I have to get over there right now. Or else Grandma is gonna get to touch it, and not me."

Then Mother looked at me very strange.

And Daddy went to get his keys.

Mother and Daddy made me take the tool belt back to the store.

They made me give it to the man.

"Here," I said. "I cannot be trusted with this wonderful thing."

The man smiled kind of sad.

"Sorry, sis,[1]" he said.

"That's okay," I said. "'Cause the nails

---

1 **sis** '아가씨' 또는 '언니'라는 뜻으로 여자아이나 젊은 여자를 부를 때 사용하는 비격식적인 호칭이다.

didn't actually work that good."

He gave me my money back.

"Maybe when you're older," he said.

"Maybe," I said. "Plus also, I might get a toilet **brush**."

After the store, I went to my grampa Miller's.

He was working in his garden.

I ran my fastest at him.

"GRAMPA MILLER! HEY, GRAMPA MILLER! DID YOU FIX IT YET? DID YOU ALREADY FIX THE TOILET?"

He **twirl**ed me around.

"Not yet!" he said. "Not yet I didn't! I've been waitin' for you!"

And so just then, me and him hurried

up.

And we got our tools.

And we runned **upstairs**.

Then we took the **lid** right off that thing!

And I **flush**ed all the water right out of it!

I touched the big ball!

"This is fun! Right, Grampa? Right? This is the time of our life!^{2}" I said.

"Sure it is! Of course it is!" said my grampa Frank Miller.

I laughed very happy.

"Hey, Grampa. Guess what? I am the *only one*!" I said.

He looked **confuse**d at me.

"I am the *only one* in Room Nine who is fixin' a toilet!" I explained.

Then Grampa Miller laughed, too. "You're really somethin'," he said.

---

2 **the time of one's life** '아주 즐거운 경험'이라는 뜻의 숙어.

"You're really somethin', too, Grampa," I said back.

Then I **hug**ged him real tight.

And I climbed up on his **lap**.

And I told him a secret in his ear.

"And guess what else?" I **whisper**ed. "I still would like a goat."